A RIVER DREAM

ALLEN SAY

Houghton Mifflin Company

Boston 1988

For Fanny and Mel Krieger

Library of Congress Cataloging-in-Publication Data

Say, Allen.
　A river dream/Allen Say.
　p. cm.
　Summary: While sick in bed, a young boy opens a box from his uncle
and embarks on a fantastical fishing trip.
　ISBN 0-395-48294-1
　[1. Fishing—Fiction. 2. Uncles—Fiction.] I. Title.
PZ7.S2744Ri　1988　　　88-14740
[E]—dc19　　　　　　　CIP
　　　　　　　　　　　AC

Printed in the United States of America

H　10　9　8　7　6　5　4　3　2　1

A RIVER DREAM

The week that Mark had a high fever, Uncle Scott sent him a small metal box for trout flies. Mark was thrilled to have his uncle's favorite fly box. And what's more, it brought back memories of his first fishing trip.

Last summer, Uncle Scott had taken him to a secret place on a sparkling river, and Mark had hooked a rainbow trout with a fly. How the little fish had jumped! More than anything else, Mark wanted to show his catch to his mother and father, but the fish got away and he never caught another.

"Better luck next time," Uncle Scott had said.

When Mark opened the box, he was startled by a cloud of mayflies that rose up from it. As the flies fluttered out the window, he looked outside and rubbed his eyes in wonder.

The whole neighborhood had disappeared! A river flowed where the street had been, and a forest spread out as far as he could see. Then he noticed the mayflies hovering over the water, and shiny fish began to leap up after them. Mark rushed outside.

He saw a rowboat bobbing in the shallow water.

"I wonder whose it is," he whispered. He looked all around but saw no one. But the mayflies had moved down the river, with the leaping fish after them.

"Well, I'm going to borrow this, just for a little while," he said and got into the boat.

As Mark drifted around the first bend in the river, he saw a lone fisherman below him.

Then, quite near Mark, a fish leapt out of the water, almost splashing him. It was the largest trout he had ever seen. It had a hook in its mouth.

"How about that, Mark!" shouted the fisherman.

"Uncle Scott!" Mark cried. "What are you doing here?"

"Funny you should ask," said Uncle, reeling in the fish. "I was about to ask what you were doing in my boat."

"This is your boat?" said Mark.

Uncle nodded. "Well, I'm glad to see you're feeling better. So, did you like the box I sent you?"

"Oh, yes, thank you very much. But you know what? All the flies flew away. I mean, they were real flies!"

"What magic!" Uncle laughed. "This fellow certainly thought my fly was real."

Uncle Scott netted the fish, removed the fly from its mouth, and let it swim away. Mark was amazed.

"Why did you do that?" asked Mark.

"Why didn't I kill the fish?" said Uncle. "I like to leave the river the way I found it. It's like cutting trees, Mark. You keep cutting trees and soon you're going to have bald mountains."

"Then why do you fish?"

"Just for the fun of it," Uncle replied. "Besides, maybe one day I will catch a mermaid. A wise old fisherman said that."

"But mermaids aren't real," said Mark.

"Aren't they?" Uncle smiled.

Mayflies began to flit all around them, and rising trout made rings on the water.

"The magic hour, my boy," said Uncle, climbing into the boat. "Do you remember your roll cast?"

"Yes, like this." Mark nodded, swinging his hand back and forth.

"Well, this may be your lucky night." Uncle handed Mark the rod.

Mark flushed with excitement. He raised the rod tip high, until the line hung behind his shoulder — just as his uncle had taught him. Then, with a quick, chopping stroke, he whipped the rod downward. The line shot out, and the cream-colored fly drifted down on the slick water like a snowflake. Mark took a deep breath.

"Fine cast!" Uncle exclaimed. "Now keep your eye on the fly. Remember, you're not going to feel the strike. You're going to see it. When you see a fish take your fly, raise your rod. Easy does it, my boy, you don't want to break your line."

Mark kept his eye on the fly, and suddenly the water swelled under it. Then a gaping mouth broke the surface and the fly was gone!

"Set the hook!" Uncle shouted.

Mark raised the rod, and the rod bent over from some heavy weight. The reel screeched as the line ran out. A large trout leapt in the air.

"It's bigger than the one you caught!" yelled Mark.

"Some rainbow!" Uncle agreed. "Let him run! Keep the rod up!"

The great trout put up a mighty fight, running again and again, leaping and twisting, but it could not break the line. When it could fight no more, Mark reeled it in. It barely fitted in Uncle's net.

"He's beautiful!" said Mark.

"Magnificent!" said Uncle. "And you're some fisherman!"

Mark sat down to admire his prize.

"Can I keep it?" he asked finally.

"Kill it, you mean?" said Uncle.

"Well . . . I want to show it to Mom and Dad. . . . It's my fish."

"That it is," said his uncle. "You must kill it quickly." He opened his knife and gave it to his nephew.

"I have to do it?" asked Mark.

"It's your fish," said Uncle, lighting his pipe.

"How?" The boy waved the knife.

"Give it a quick stab there." Uncle Scott pointed at the rainbow's head. "Mind your hand, it's very sharp."

Mark stared at the gasping fish, then at the gleaming blade.

The knife dropped from Mark's hand with a loud clatter. Then he lifted his catch with both hands and lowered it into the river. The limp fish did not move.

"Is it dead?" asked Mark.

"It'll be all right," said his uncle. "Rock it back and forth and let water go through the gills."

So Mark rocked the fish, back and forth, back and forth — until the fins began to wave. Then the sleek fish stirred, as though waking from a long sleep. With a flick of its tail the rainbow slipped out of the boy's hands, and the boy watched his trout swim away.

"That was fun," he whispered.

"So what's the use in fishing if you don't keep any fish?"
Uncle Scott asked.

"Oh, it's good to leave the river the way I found it," said Mark.
"Besides, I might catch a mermaid some day."

"That's my man," Uncle said, laughing. "Just for that I'm going
to build you a rod."

"A rod like yours?" shouted Mark.

"Exactly like mine, with your name on it," said Uncle.

Just then they heard someone talking quite nearby.

"Sounds like a woman," said Uncle Scott. "Maybe that *was*
your mermaid."

They looked upstream and saw a house. All the windows were
lit except for Mark's. It was still open, and his mother's voice drifted
out of it.

"I've kept you out long enough," Uncle Scott said and took the oars.

Mark said good night to his uncle and climbed into his room through the window. A short while later, when his parents opened the door, Mark pretended to be fast asleep.

"Leave it to my brother," Mother whispered. "Sending fishing lures to a sick child. Why, they're all over the bed. He could have hurt himself!"

"Look," said his father. "His temperature seems almost normal."

"Thank goodness," said his mother.

And Mark fell asleep.